This book belongs to

ciaran Jhon Andrew
Barres / Josh

This edition published by Parragon in 2011

Parragon
Queen Street House
4 Queen Street
Bath BA1 1HE, UK
www.paragon.com

ISBN 978-1-4454-2680-8

Printed in China

THE
LION KING

Bath · New York · Singapore · Hong Kong · Cologne · Delhi
Melbourne · Amsterdam · Johannesburg · Auckland · Shenzhen

The hot African sun rose on an amazing sight. Giraffes, zebras, elephants and animals of all kinds were gathered at Pride Rock. This was an important day.

King Mufasa and Queen Sarabi watched as Rafiki, the wise baboon, presented their newborn son to the kingdom. The animals cheered and bowed before Prince Simba.

But one family member didn't attend the celebration – Mufasa's brother, Scar. Scar was angry that he was no longer next in line to be king.

Mufasa and his assistant, Zazu, went to ask Scar why he had missed the presentation of Simba.

"Oh, it must have slipped my mind," Scar sneered and he walked away.

Simba grew into a playful and curious cub. Early one morning, Mufasa brought Simba to the top of Pride Rock. "Everything that the light touches is our kingdom," he told his son. "One day the sun will set on my time here and will rise with you as the new king."

"Wow!" cried Simba. "But what about that shadowy place?"

"You must never go across the border, Simba," said Mufasa sternly.

"But I thought a king can do whatever he wants," said Simba. Mufasa explained. "There's more to being king than getting your way all the time. You need to respect all creatures. We are all connected in the great Circle of Life."

Simba tried to listen but he was busy chasing grasshoppers and practicing his pounce.

Just then, Zazu arrived with important news. Hyenas had crossed into the Pride Lands!

Mufasa ordered Zazu to take Simba home and ran off to battle the hyenas.

"I never get to go anywhere," Simba complained.

Back at home, Simba went to see his uncle Scar.

"My dad just showed me the whole kingdom," the cub bragged. "And I'm gonna rule it all!"

"Did he show you that place beyond the border?" asked Scar slyly. "Only the bravest of lions would dare go to an elephant graveyard."

Simba didn't see his uncle's evil trap. He decided to show his father what a brave cub he could be.

Simba set out to find his best friend, Nala. She was lying with their mothers on a rock nearby. "Mum, can Nala and I go to this great place...near the water hole?" fibbed Simba.

"As long as Zazu goes with you," answered Sarabi.

"We've got to ditch Zazu!" Simba whispered to Nala. "We're really going to an elephant graveyard!"

Simba and Nala laughed as they ran in and out of animal herds to escape from Zazu. "We lost him!" cried Nala.

Together they played, tumbling and rolling. With a thump, they landed next to a huge elephant skull.

Zazu caught up with them, but it was too late. Banzai, Shenzi and Ed, three drooling hyenas with sharp teeth, surrounded them!

The hyenas grabbed Zazu first. "Why don't you pick on somebody your own size?" shouted Simba.

Then one tried to catch Nala, but Simba swiped his claws across the hyena's cheek.

Suddenly, a tremendous roar shook the ground. It was Mufasa!

His giant paw struck one of the hyenas as he growled, "If you ever come near my son again..." The hyenas ran away before he could finish.

Mufasa scolded his son on the way home. "You disobeyed me, Simba."

"I was just trying to be brave, like you, Dad," said Simba softly.

"Being brave doesn't mean you go looking for trouble," replied Mufasa.

Then Mufasa told Simba how the kings of the past look down from the stars above. "They will always be there to guide you...and so will I."

Scar was angry when the hyenas told him that Simba had escaped. But he quickly came up with a new plan to get rid of Simba and his father.

"I will be king!" he cried.

The next day, Scar found Simba. "Your father has a surprise for you," he said. Scar led Simba down a steep gorge and told him to wait there.

Then Scar signalled the hyenas to frighten a herd of wildebeests. The panicked animals stampeded right toward Simba! Hearing the thunder of hooves, Mufasa looked into the gorge and saw his son. He leaped down and saved Simba's life.

Simba was safe, but Mufasa was still in danger. As he tried to climb away from the stampede, the rocks crumbled beneath him.

Struggling up the cliff, Mufasa saw Scar. "Brother, help me!" he cried.

Scar dug his sharp claws into Mufasa's paws and whispered, "Long live the king!" Then he let Mufasa go, and Mufasa fell, disappearing beneath the herd below.

Simba had seen only that his father had fallen. When the stampede was gone, Simba ran to Mufasa. He tried to wake him, but the Lion King was dead.

"Help!" cried Simba.

Scar came to Simba's side. "If it weren't for you," he said, "your father would still be alive! Run away and never return!"

Heartbroken, poor Simba ran away as fast as he could.

Scar sent the hyenas out to kill Simba, but the cub escaped them once more.

Scar was certain that Simba was dead. He went back to Pride Rock and told everyone the news. "It is with a heavy heart," he lied, "that I become your new king!"

Everyone in the Pride Lands mourned for their beloved king and Simba.

Meanwhile, Simba was far away from the Pride Lands. The ground turned dry and cracked beneath him. The hot sun beat down as vultures circled above his head.

Exhausted and unable to go any farther, Simba slumped to the ground.

After a long while, Simba awoke. Everything around him looked different. There were trees and grass and flowers instead of desert.

A meerkat named Timon and a warthog named Pumbaa had brought him to their home. "You nearly died," said Pumbaa.

"We saved you!" cried Timon. Thanking them, Simba stood up and started to leave.

Pumbaa asked Simba where he was from, but Simba didn't want to answer. "I did something terrible...but I don't want to talk about it."

"You gotta put your troubles behind you, kid," said Timon. "No past, no future, no worries...hakuna matata!" Simba decided to stay with his new friends.

Years passed and Simba grew into a young lion, and had lots of fun with his friends Timon and Pumbaa.

One night while looking up at the stars, Simba remembered his father's words. "Someone once told me that the great kings of the past are up there, watching over us," he said to his friends.

The next day, Pumbaa was chasing a bug when a fierce lioness sprang at him from the tall grass. He screamed and ran away, but got stuck beneath a fallen tree.

"She's gonna eat me!" he squealed. Simba heard his friend's cries and rushed to help.

Simba wrestled with the lioness, but then realized she was his old friend Nala. "You're alive!" she said happily. "That means you're the king!"

Nala told Simba how Scar had destroyed the Pride Lands. "Simba, if you don't do something, everyone will starve."

"I can't go back," said Simba angrily, and he turned and walked away.

Simba thought about what Nala had said. "I won't go back," he said to himself. "It won't change anything." Just then, Simba heard a chanting song from the jungle.

Rafiki the baboon came walking toward him. "If you want to see your father again, look down there," Rafiki said, pointing into the pool of water next to them.

Simba saw the face of his father staring back at him. "You see?" said Rafiki. "He lives in you!"

Now Simba looked up and saw his father's face in the stars and heard his voice. "Look inside yourself, Simba. Remember who you are...you are my son and the one true king."

The next morning Rafiki found Nala, Timon and Pumbaa. He told them that Simba had returned to the Pride Lands. "He's gone back to challenge his uncle!" cheered Nala.

When Simba reached the Pride Lands, he was saddened by what he saw. His homeland that was once green and beautiful had turned barren under Scar's rule.

Bravely, Simba continued on his journey.

When Simba arrived at Pride Rock, he let out a roar that shook the earth. Scar was surprised and frightened. He thought the hyenas had killed Simba long ago.

"This is my kingdom!" shouted Simba. "Step down, Scar." Scar ordered his hyenas to attack. They surrounded Simba and drove him to the edge of a cliff.

Simba grabbed onto the rocks with his claws as Scar stood above him. "That's just the way your father looked before I killed him," snarled Scar.

Then Simba realized that it had been Scar who killed his father. With new strength, Simba lunged onto the rock and attacked.

At that moment, Nala, Timon and Pumbaa arrived and a battle broke out on Pride Rock.

This time, Simba trapped Scar at the steep edge of Pride Rock. Sparing his life, he ordered his uncle to run away and never return. Scar pretended to leave, but then turned and lunged at Simba. Simba swiped his great claw and Scar fell to his death in the gorge below.

Simba took his rightful place as the Lion King and once again the land flourished. Soon all the animals gathered at Pride Rock to celebrate the birth of Simba and Nala's cub. The Circle of Life would continue.

The End